Johann Reinhold Forster

Forsters Animals of Hudsons Bay

Johann Reinhold Forster

Forsters Animals of Hudsons Bay

ISBN/EAN: 9783337816209

Printed in Europe, USA, Canada, Australia, Japan

Cover: Foto ©Raphael Reischuk / pixelio.de

More available books at **www.hansebooks.com**

THE WILLUGHBY SOCIETY.

FORSTER'S
ANIMALS OF HUDSON'S BAY.

EDITED BY

PHILIP LUTLEY SCLATER, M.A., Ph. D., F.R.S.

LONDON:

1882

𝕮𝖆𝖒𝖇𝖗𝖎𝖉𝖌𝖊 :
PRINTED BY C. J. CLAY AND SON,
AT THE UNIVERSITY PRESS.

PREFACE.

THE present essay, reprinted from the sixty-second volume of the "Philosophical Transactions," was, like the "Faunula Americana," no doubt written by FORSTER during his temporary residence in this country before his departure with Cook on his second voyage.

The circumstances which led to its preparation are explained in the following paragraph, which is attached to the corresponding paper on the Quadrupeds of Hudson's Bay (*Phil. Trans.* LXII. p. 370).

"Among the occasional advantages, which the observations "of the late Transit of Venus have procured, that of receiving "useful informations from, and settling correspondencies in, "several parts of the world, is not the least considerable. "From the factory at Hudson's Bay, the Royal Society were "favoured with a large collection of uncommon quadrupeds, "birds, fishes, &c., together with some account of their names, "place of abode, manner of life, uses, by Mr Graham, a gentle-"man belonging to the settlement on Severn River; and the "Governors of the Hudson's Bay Company have most obligingly "sent orders, that these communications should be from time to "time continued."

"The descriptions contained in the following papers were "prepared and given by Mr Forster, before his departure on an "expedition, which will probably open an ample field to the "most important discoveries."

Of the eight birds described and named as new by Forster at the end of this memoir, six, according to the most recent authorities on North American birds, are entitled to remain under Forster's designation, namely,

Falco sacer, Forst. = *Hierofalco gyrfalco var. sacer* (Forst.)
Strix nebulosa, Forst. = *Syrnium nebulosum* (Forst.)
Emberiza leucophrys, Forst. = *Zonotrichia leucophrys* (Forst.)
Muscicapa striata, Forst. = *Dendrœca striata* (Forst.)
Parus hudsonicus, Forst. = *Parus hudsonicus* (Forst.)
Scolopax borealis, Forst. = *Numenius borealis* (Forst.)

But it has been pointed out to me by Prof. Newton, and, I think, correctly, that the species described by Forster as *Falco sacer* is not the American form of *Hierofalco gyrfalco* as commonly supposed, but *Astur atricapillus*.

Of the remaining two species described in the Appendix, *Fringilla hudsonias* of Forster is usually identified with *Junco hyemalis* (Linn.), and his *Anas nivalis* with *Anser hyperboreus* (Pallas).

Falco spadiceus, shortly mentioned as a new species in the first part of the memoir (p. 383), is commonly referred to *Circus hudsonius* (Linn.).

P. L. S.

11, HANOVER SQUARE, LONDON, W.
March 21st, 1882.

XXIX. *An Account of the Birds sent from* Hudson's Bay; *with Observations relative to their Natural History*; *and* Latin *Descriptions of some of the most uncommon.* *By* J. R. Forster, *F. R. S.*

Read June 18—25, 1772.

I. Land-Birds.

1. { Accipitres
     { Rapacious.   Faun. Am. Sept.

1. Falco,} 1. Columbarius. 128. 21. Pigeon Hawk.
Falcon.} Faun. Am. Sept. p. 9.   Catesby I. t. 3.
Epervier de la Caroline.   Brisson I. p. 378.

Severn river, N° 19.

> This species is called a *small-bird hawk* at Hudson's Bay.   It is migratory, arriving near Severn River in May, breeding on the coast, and then retiring to a warmer climate in autumn.   It feeds on small birds; and, on the approach of any person, will fly in circles, making a hideous shrieking noise. The breast
> and

and belly are yellowish, with brown streaks, which are not mentioned by the ornithologists, though their descriptions answer in other respects. It weighs six ounces and a half, its length is 10½, the breadth 22½. Catesby's figure is a very indifferent one.

FALCO, 2. Spadiceus. *New Species.* Chocolate Falcon. Faun. Am. Sept. p. 9.

This species, at first sight, bears some resemblance to the European Moor Buzzard, or *Aeruginosus*, Linn. but is much less, and wants the light spots on the head and shoulders. No number or description was sent along with it.

FALCO, 3. Sacer, Brisson, I. p. 377. Sacre ·de Buffon, Oiseaux, (edition in 12mo.) Tom. II. p. 349. t. 14. Faun. Am. Sept. p. 9.
Severn River, N° 16.

Speckled Partridge Hawk, at Hudson's Bay. The name is derived from its feeding on the birds of the Grous tribe, commonly called partridges, at Hudson's Bay. Its irides are yellow, and the legs blue. It comes nearest the *Sacre* of Brisson, Buffon, and Belon; but Buffon says it has black eyes, which is very indistinct; for the irides are black in none of the falcons, and in few other birds; and the pupil, if he means that, is black in all birds. It is said, by Belon, to come from Tartary and Russia, and is, therefore, probably a northern bird. It is very voracious
and

(3)

and bold, catching partridges out of a covey,
which the Europeans are driving into their
nests. It breeds in April and May. Its
young are ready to fly in the middle of June.
Its nests, as those of all other falcons, are
built in unfrequented places; therefore, the
author of the account from Severn River
could not ascertain how many eggs it lays;
however, the Indians told him it commonly
lay two. It never migrates, and weighs
$2\frac{1}{2}$ pounds; its length is 22 inches, its breadth
3 feet.

2. STRIX, } 4. Brachyotos. The short-eared Owl.
 Owl. } Brit. Zoology, folio, plate B. 3. octavo,
 I. p. 156. Faun. Am. Sept. 9.
Severn River, N° 17 and 64.

Mouse Hawk at Hudson's Bay. It answers the
description and figure in the British Zoology;
but its ears or long feathers do not appear.
The smallness of the head has, probably,
given occasion to call it a hawk, though it
does not fly about in quest of prey, like
other hawks (as the account from Severn
River says); it sits quiet on the stumps of
trees, waiting mice with all the attention of
a domestic cat, being an inveterate enemy
of those little animals. It migrates southward in autumn; and breeds along the coast.
Its irides are yellow. Its weight is 14 ounces;
its length 16 inches, the breadth 3 feet.

STRIX

STRIX, 5. Nyctea. 132. 6. Snowy Owl. Faun. Am. Sept. 9.

Churchill River, N° 7. White Owl.

It seems to be in its winter dress, as it is intirely white. The feet are covered with long white hair-like feathers to the very nails, but there are none on the soles or under parts of the toes.

STRIX, 6. Funerea. 133. 11. Canada Owl. Faun. Am. Sept. 9.

Severn River, N° 13. Churchill River, N° 11.

Cabeticuch, or *Cabaducutch,* is the Indian name of this bird. Linneus's description answers perfectly. The male, which in the class of birds of prey is generally smaller, is, however, in this species, larger than the female, according to the account from Severn River. Its colour is likewise much blacker, and the spots more distinct. The eyes are large and prominent; the irides of a bright yellow. The weight is 12 ounces; its length 17 inches, the breadth 2 feet. It has only two young at one hatching.

STRIX, 7. Passerina. 133. 12. Little Owl. Brit. Zool. Faun. Am. Sept. 9.

(The number belonging to this bird is lost, but it is most probably that from Severn River, N° 15. called *Shipomospish* by the natives).

The crown of the head is speckled with white, as in the *Strix funerca.*

VOL. LXII. D d d STRIX,

STRIX, 8. Nebulosa. *New species.* The grey Owl. Severn River, N° 36.

> This fine non-descript owl lives upon hares, ptarmigans, mice, &c. It has two young at a time. The specimen sent over is said to be one of the largest. It is not described by any author. Its weight is 3 pounds, length 16 inches, breadth 4 feet.

3. LANIUS,} 9. Excubitor. 135. 11. Great Butcher-
   Shrike.} bird. Brit. Zool. Cinereous Shrike.
   Faun. Am. Sept.
Severn River, N° 11.

> *White Whiskijohn* at Hudson's Bay. The specimen is a male; it weighs two ounces and a half, is seldom found on the coast, but frequent about a hundred miles inland; and feeds on small birds. It corresponds with ours in every respect.

II. { Picæ.
    { Pies.   Faun. Am. Sept.

4. CORVUS,} 10. Canadensis. 158. 16. Cinereous
   Crow.} Crow. Faun. Am. Sept. 9.
Severn River, N° 9 and 10.

> These birds are called *Whiskijohn* and *Whiskijack* at the Hudson's Bay. They weigh 2 ounces; and are 9 inches long, and 11 broad. Their eyes are black, and their feet of the same colour. Their characters correspond with the Linnean description. They breed early in spring; their nests are made of sticks and
> > grass,

grass, and built in pine trees; they have two, rarely three, young ones at a time; their eggs are blue; they fly in pairs; the male and female are perfectly alike; they feed on black moss, worms, and even flesh. When near habitations or tents, they are apt to pilfer every thing they can come at, even salt meat; they are bold, and come into the tents to eat victuals out of the dishes. They watch persons baiting the traps for martins, and devour the bait as soon as they turn their backs. These birds lay up stores for the winter, and are seldom seen in January, unless near habitations; they are a kind of mock-bird; when caught, they pine away and die, though their appetite never fails them.

CORVUS, 11. Pica. 157. 13. Magpie. Brit. Zool. Faun. Am. Sept. 9.

Albany Fort, N° 5.

It is called *Oue-ta-kee-aske*, i. e. *Heart-bird*, by the Indians. It is a bird of passage, and rarely seen; it agrees, in all respects, with the European magpie, upon comparison.

5. PICUS, } 12. Auratus. 174. 9. Gold-wing Woodpecker. } Woodpecker. Faun. Am. Sept. 10. Catesby, I. 18.

Albany Fort, N° 4. the large Woodpecker.

The natives of America call this bird *Ou-thee-quan-nor-now*, from the yellow colour of the shafts of the quill and underside of the tail feathers. It is a bird of passage; visits the

D d d 2   neigh-

neighbourhood of Albany Fort in April, leaves it in September; lays from four to six eggs in hollow trees, feeds on small worms and other insects. Its descriptions answer exactly.

PICUS, 13. Villosus, 175. 16. Hairy Woodpecker. Faun. Am. Sept. 10. Catesby I. 19.

Severn River, Nº 56.

> The specimen sent over is a female, by its wanting the red on the head. The descriptions of Linneus and Brisson agree; only the two middlemost feathers are black, the next are of the same colour, but have a white rhomboidal spot near the tip; the next are black, with the upper half obliquely white, the very tip being black; the next after that are white, with a round black spot on the inner side close to the base, and the lower part of the shaft is black, the outermost feathers are quite white, the shaft only at the base being black.

14. Tridactylus. 177. 21. Three-toïd Woodpecker. Faun. Am. Sept.

Severn River, Nº 8.

> A female, weight 2 ounces, length 8 inches, breadth 13; eyes dark blue, legs black. It builds its nest in trees, lives in woods upon worms picked out of trees, is not very common at Severn River. The descriptions answer.

III. Gallinæ.

III. $\begin{cases} \text{Gallinæ.} \\ \text{Gallinaceous.} \quad \text{Faun. Am. Sept.} \end{cases}$

6. Tetrao. $\begin{cases} 15\,\text{Canadensis}, 274.\,3. \\ \text{Canace}, 275.\,7. \end{cases}$ $\begin{cases} \text{Faun. Am. Sept. 10.} \\ \text{Spotted Grous.} \end{cases}$
Grous.
Gelinotte du Canada, male et femelle, Pl. enl.
131 et 132. Buffon Oiseaux II. p. 279. 4to.
Brisson I. p. 203. t. 20. f. 1, 2, and p. 201. app.
10. Edwards, t. 118 and 71.

Severn River, N° 5. Woodpartridge.

These birds are all the year long at Hudson's
Bay, and never change the colour of their
plumage. The accounts from Hudson's Bay
say, there is no material difference between
the male and female ; which must be a mistake, as they are really very different. Linneus's descriptions of the Tetrao Canadensis,
and Canace, both answer to the specimens sent
over, so that, after comparing them, I find
they are only one and the same species. I
suppose the dividing them into two, was oc-
casioned by Brisson's and Edwards's descriptions, being taken from specimens sent from
different parts of the continent of America,
and perhaps caught at different seasons. Mr.
de Buffon has, I find, the same opinion with
me, and by comparing the drawings of Edwards, with those of the Planches enluminées,
it is put beyond a doubt. These birds are
very stupid, may be knocked down with a
stick, and are frequently caught by the natives

I

tives with a stick and a loop. In summer
they are good eating ; but in winter they taste
strongly of the pine spruce, upon which they
feed during that season, eating berries in summer. They live in pine woods, their nests ·
are on the ground ; they generally lay but five
eggs.

Tetrao, 16. Lagopus, 274. 4. White Grous. Faun.
    Am. Sept. 10. Ptarmigan. Br. Zool. La-
    gopéde de la Baye de Hudson. Buffon Ois-
    eaux II. p. 276. Edw. t. 72.

Severn River, N° 1—4. Willow-partridges.

The Hudson's Bay ptarmigan has been separated
from the European in the British Zoology, and
afterwards by M. de Buffon : however, I must
own, I cannot yet find the differences which
they assign to these species. They contend that
the Hudson's Bay bird figured by Edwards is
twice as big as the European ptarmigan ; Mr.
Edwards, I think, does not intimate this,
when he says, the bird is of a middle size,
between partridge and pheasant ; he on the
contrary supposes them to be the same species.
The British Zoology, after Willoughby, says,
the ptarmigan's length is $13\frac{3}{4}$ inches. The
account from Severn River says it is 16 inches.
The breadth in the British Zoology is said to
be 23 inches. The breadth in the Hudson's
Bay birds, according to the accounts from Severn River, is 23 inches. Willoughby's ptarmigan weighed 14 ounces ; that in the British
                               Zool.

Zool. illustr. t. 13. 19 ounces; that from the
Hudson's Bay (1½℔) 24 ounces. These differences are of little consequence, and far
from increasing the Hudson's Bay bird to
double the size of the European. The British Zoology says, there is a difference in
the summer colours; but Mr. Edwards in-
forms us, that he compared the Hudson's Bay
bird with the descriptions of former ornithologists, and found them to answer; he likewise assures us he had the same bird from
Norway. Therefore I cannot help dissenting
from the British Zoology, in this one parti-
cular, and thinking with Linneus and Brisson,
that the European and Hudson's Bay ptarmigans are the same, especially as the colours
vary very much in the different sexes and at
different seasons. To this we may add the
testimony of a gentleman well versed in
natural history, who, having had opportunities
of comparing numbers of Hudson's Bay and
European ptarmigans, assured me that he did
not see any difference between them. They
go together in great flocks in the beginning of
October, living among the willows, of which
they eat the tops (whence they have got the
name of willow partridges): about that time
they lose their beautiful summer plumage,
and exchange it for a snowy white dress,
most providently adapted by its thickness to
screen them against the severity of the season, and by its colour against their enemies
the

the hawks and owls, against whose attacks they would otherwise find no shelter. Each feather is double, that is, a short one under a long one, to keep them warm. In the latter end of March, they begin again to change their plumage, and have got their full summer dress by the end of June. They breed every where along the coast, and have from nine to eleven young at a time; making their nests on the ground, generally on dry ridges. They are excellent eating, and so plentiful that ten thousand have been taken at Severn, York, and Churchill Forts. The method of netting or catching them, is as follows: a net made of jack-twine, twenty feet square, is laced to four long poles, and supported in front with the sticks, in a perpendicular situation; a long line is fastened to these supports, one end of it reaching to a place where a person lies concealed; several men drive the ptarmigans (which are as tame as chickens, especially on a mild, snowy day), towards the net, which they run to, as soon as they see it. The person concealed draws the· line, by which means the net falls down, and catches 50 or 70 ptarmigans at once. They are sometimes rather wild, but grow better humoured (as Mr. Graham says) by being driven about, for they seldom forsake those willows which they have once frequented.

TETRAO.

TETRAO. 17. Togatus, 275. 8. Shoulder-knot
Grous. Grosse Gelinotte du Canada. Pl. enl. 104.
Briss. I. 207. t. 21. f. 1. Buffon Oiseaux II. p.
287.

Severn River, N° 60 and 61. Albany Fort 1 and 2.

This bird answers the descriptions given of it by
the ornithologists in all respects, and perfectly
resembles the figure in Brisson, and in the
Planches enluminées. It differs from Edwards's ruffed heathcock, t. 248. or Linneus's Tetrao umbellus, as the latter has
not the shining black axillar feathers, or
shoulder-knot, but a ferruginous one, is much
less, and has brighter colours. M. de Buffon, however, thinks they are the same,
and suspects at the same time, that the bird
which he calls la grosse Gelinotte du Canada
(and which is the same with the Society's
specimens) is the female of Mr. Edwards's
bird, t. 248. This conjecture is destroyed
by the specimens now sent from Hudson's
Bay, which by the accounts from thence are
expressly said to be males. The shoulder-
knot grouses bear the Indian name of *Puskee*,
or *Puspuskee*, at Hudson's Bay, on account
of the leanness and dryness of their flesh,
which is extremely white, and of a very close
texture, but when well prepared is excellent
eating. They are pretty common at Moose
Fort and Henly House, but are seldom seen
at Albany Fort, or to the northward of the
above places. In winter they feed upon ju-

VOL. LXII. E e e niper

niper tops, in summer on goose-berries, rasp-
berries, currants, cranberries, &c. They are
not migratory, staying all the year at Moose
Fort; they build their nests on dry ground,
hatch nine young at a time, to which the
mother clucks, as our common hen does;
and on the least appearance of danger, or in
order to enjoy a comfortable degree of warmth,
the young ones retire under the wings of their
parent.

N.B. A specimen, which is supposed to be
either a young bird or a female, wants the
blueish black shoulder-knot; but it is the
same in all other respects.

TETRAO, 18. Phasianellus. Linn. Syst. Nat. Ed.
X. p. 160. n. 5. Edw. 117. Longtailed Grous.
Faun. Am. Septentr. 10.

Severn River, N° 6 and 7. Albany Fort, N° 3.

This bird, which Mr. Edwards has drawn plate
117, was by Linneus in the tenth edition of
his System, ranged as a new species of grous
or tetrao, by the specific name of Phasianellus (alluding to the name of Pheasant which
it bears at Hudson's Bay, and likewise to its
pointed tail). He afterwards in the new or
twelfth edition of the System, p. 273. makes
it a variety of the great Cock of the Wood,
or Tetrao Urogallus, probably from the account in Mr. Edwards, that the male struts
very upright, is in general of a darker colour
than the female, and has a glossy neck. These
circumstances, howevere, are not sufficient to
bring

bring them under the same species, for it is known that the males of all the grous tribe, and indeed of most of the gallinaceous birds, are used to strut in a very stately manner, and that the colours of their plumage are much more distinct than those of the females. But the specific difference alone, which Linneus assigns to the cock of the wood, absolutely excludes our Hudson's Bay species; he calls it Tetrao pedibus hirsutis, cauda rotundata, axillis albis. Whoever examines Mr. Edwards's figure, and the specimens now in the Society's possession, will find the tail very short, but pointed, the two middle feathers being half an inch longer than the rest, (Mr. Edwards says two inches) and the axillæ, or shoulders, by no means white: besides this difference, the colour and size of the Hudson's Bay bird are likewise vastly different from those of the cock of the wood. Its length is 17 inches, its breadth 24, and, as Mr. Edwards justly says, it is somewhat bigger than the common pheasant. The great cock of the wood is as big as a turky; and its female, which is much less, however far exceeds our bird, it being 26 inches long, and 40 broad. See British Zool. octavo, p. 200. The figures given of the female of the T. Urogallus, or great cock of the wood, in the Br. Zool. folio, plate M*, and the Planche enlumineé 75, will serve upon comparison as a convincing proof of the vast difference there is between the Hudson's Bay pheasant grous and the European cock

E e e 2   of

of the wood. The figure, which Mr. Edwards has given of the former bird, does not exactly correspond with the Society's specimen, as he has represented the marks on the breast half-moon shaped, though they are heart-shaped as those on the belly in the dried bird; that is, they are white spots, with a pale brownish yellow cordated brim. Nor can I agree with Mr. Edwards, when he calls this bird the long-tailed grous from Hudson's Bay; for its tail is really very short, in comparison with that of other grouse, and its smallness and acuteness afford one of the most distinguishing characters of the species.

The native Indians call these pheasant grouses, *Oc-kiss-cow:* they are found all the year long, amongst the small juniper bushes, of which the buds are their principal food, as also the buds of birch in winter, and all sorts of berries in summer. They never vary their colours; nor is there any great difference between the male and female, except in the caruncula or comb over the eye, which in the male is an inch long, and ⅜ of an inch high. The account from Albany Fort adds, that the colour of the male is somewhat browner, and almost a chocolate on the breast. Their flesh is of a light brown, exceeding juicy, and they are very plump. They lay from 9 to 13 eggs; their young can run almost as soon as they are hatched; they make a piping noise somewhat like a chicken. The cock has a shrill crowing note, not very loud;

I   but

but when disturbed, or whilst flying, he makes a repeated noise of cuck, cock. They are most common in winter at Albany Fort.

Before I leave the genus of grouses, I must observe that their feet have a peculiarity, taken notice of by few authors; the toes, in several species, have on each side a row of short flexible teeth, like those of a comb; so that the toes appear pectinated. The species, which are known to have such pectinated toes, are,

1. The great Cock of the Wood, *Tetrao Urogallus*, Linn.

2. The Black Cock, *T. Tetrix*, Linn.

3. The Spotted Grous, $\begin{cases} T.\ Canadensis, \\ T.\ Canace, \text{ Linn.} \end{cases}$ and

4. The Ruffed Grous, *T. Umbellus*, Linn.

5. The Shoulder-knot Grous, *T. Togatus*, Linn.

6. The Pheasant Grous, *T. Phasianellus*.

7. The Hazel Hen, *T. Bonasia*, Linn.

8. The Pyrenæan Grous, *T. Alchata*, Linn.

This is a circumstance, which ought to be attended to in all other species of grouses, as it may in time afford a distinguishing character for a division in this great genus; the ptarmigan, or *T. Lagopus*, Linn. is without these teeth.

IV. Co-

IV. $\begin{cases} \text{Columbæ.} \\ \text{Columbine.} \quad \text{Faun. Am. Sept.} \end{cases}$

7. COLUMBA, $\big\}$ 19. Migratoria. 285. 36. Migratory
    Pigeon. $\big\}$ Pigeon. Catesb. I. 23. Kalm II.
p. 82. t. Passenger Pigeon, Faun. Am. Sept. 11.

Severn River, N° 63. Wood-pigeon.

> These pigeons are very scarce so far northward as
> Severn river, but abound near Moose-fort, and
> further inland to the southward. Their com-
> mon food are berries and juniper buds in
> winter; they fly about in great flocks, and
> are reckoned good eating. This account is
> confirmed by Kalm in his travels (English
> edition) Vol. II. p. 82 and 311. They hatch
> only two eggs at a time, and their nests are
> built in trees. Their eyes are small and black,
> the irides yellow, the feet red : the neck fine-
> ly glossed with purple, brighter in the male.
> They weigh 9 ounces.

V. $\begin{cases} \text{Passeres.} \\ \text{Passerine.} \quad \text{Faun. Am. Sept.} \end{cases}$

8. Alauda. $\big\}$ 20. Alpestris. 289. 10. Klein, Hist. of
    Lark. $\big\}$ Birds, 4to. p. 73. Shore Lark, Faun.
Am. Sept. 12. Catesb. I. 32.

Albany Fort, N° 6.

> This species is indifferently described by Linneus,
> who says that all the tail-feathers on their in-
> ner web are white, (*rectricibus dimidio in-
> teriore albis*); though it does not appear that
> he saw a specimen of it himself. Both the
> quill

quill and tail-feathers are dusky, and in both
the outermost feather only has a white exterior margin. The coverts of the tail are of
a pale ferruginous colour, and two of them
are nearly as long as the tail itself. The sca-
pulars are ferruginous; in the male, the head
and whole back have a tinge of the same colour, marked with dusky streaks; in the female, the back is grey, and the dusky stripes
of a darker hue. The crown of the head is
black in the male, dusky in the female; the
forehead is yellow, the bill and feet are black,
the belly of a dirty reddish white. These
larks are migratory, they visit the environs
of Albany Fort in the beginning of May,
but go further northward to breed: they feed
on grass-seeds, and buds of the sprig-birch;
run into small holes, and keep close to the
ground, from whence the natives give them
the name of *Chi-chup-pi-sue.*

9. Turdus. ⎱ 21. Migratorius, 292. 6. American
   Thrush. ⎰ Fieldfare. Kalm II. p. 90. Faun. Am.
   Sept. II. Catesby I. 29.

Severn River, N° 59. Albany Fort, 7, 8, 9.

The descriptions of these birds in various authors
coincide with the specimens; at Severn River
they appear at the beginning of May, and
leave the environs before the frost sets in.
At Moose Fort, in the north latitude 51°.
they build their nest, lay their eggs, and hatch
their young in the space of fourteen days;
but at York fort and Severn settlement this is
done

done in 26 days : they build their nests in trees, lay four beautiful light-blue eggs, feed on worms and carrion : when at liberty they sing very prettily, but confined in a cage, they lose their melody. There is no material distinction between the male and female. Their weight is 2½ ounces, the length 9 inches, and the breadth 1 foot ; they are called red birds at Hudson's Bay ; their Indian name is *Pee-pee-chue.*

Turdus, 22.

Severn River, N° 54 and 55, male and female.

From the striking similarity with our blackbird, the English at Hudson's Bay have given this bird the same name. However, upon a close examination, I find the difference very great between our European blackbird, and the Hudson's Bay or American one. The plumage of the male, instead of being deep black without any gloss, as in ours, has a shining purple cast, not unlike the plumage of the *Gracula Quiscula,* Linn. or shining Gracule, Faun. Am. Sept. ; or the Maize thief, of Kalm. The female indeed is very like our female blackbird, being of a dusky colour on the back, and a dark grey on the breast. The feet and bill are quite black in both sexes ; the former have the back claw almost as long again as any of the other claws. There are no vestiges of yellow palpebræ in either the male or the female ; the bill in both is strong, smooth, and subulated ; the
upper

upper mandible being carinated, but very
little arched, and without any tooth or in-
denture whatever, on the lower side. The
nostrils are as in other thrushes. This bird
has no bristles at the base of its bill, its feet
have such segments as Scopoli in the Annus
I. Historico-Naturalis attributes to the stares.
Instead of being solitary and living retired
like the European blackbirds, these American
ones come in flocks to Severn River in June,
live among the willows, build in all kinds of
trees, and return to the southward in autumn.
They feed on worms and maggots; their
weight is 2¼ ounces, and they are nine inches
long, and one foot broad. One that was
kept twelve months in a cage pined away,
and died. Notwithstanding these circumstances, I cannot help remaining undetermined
with regard to this bird, which at first sight
is like the blackbird, has the bill of a thrush,
and the feet and gregarious nature of a stare.
It is to be hoped, that future accounts from
Hudson's Bay may inform us further, of
the nature of this bird, its time of incuba-
tion, the number of eggs it lays, and the
colour of those eggs, together with the note
of the bird, the difference and characteristick
marks of both the male and female, and
other circumstances, which may serve to de-
termine to what genus and species we are to
refer this bird.

10. Loxia, { 23. Curvirostra, 299. 1. Crossbill.
Grosbeak. { Br. Zool. Faun. Am. Sept. 11. The
small variety.

Severn River, N° 27 and 28.

This bird comes to Severn River the latter end
of May, breeds more to the northward, and
returns in autumn, in its way to the south, de-
parting at the setting in of the frost. The
irides in the male are of a beautiful red, in
the female yellow: the weight is said to be
10 ounces (probably by mistake for 1 ounce,
as it is impossible so small a bird should weigh
more), the length is 6 inches, the breadth 10.

24. Enucleator, 299. 3. Pine Grosbeak. Br. Zool.
and Faun. Am. Sept. Edw. 123, 124. Pl. enl.
135. f. 1.

Severn River, N° 29, 30.

It answers to the descriptions and figures of the
ornithologists pretty well; only Edwards's female has the red too bright, which is rather
orange in our specimen, on the head, neck,
and coverts of the tail. This bird only visits
the Hudson's Bay settlements in May, on its
way to the north, and is not observed to return in autumn; its food consists of birch-
willow buds, and others of the same nature;
it weighs 2 ounces, is 9 inches long, and
13 broad.

11. Em-

11. EMBERIZA. $\begin{cases} 25. & \text{Nivalis.} & 308. & 1. & \text{Greater} \\ & \text{Brambling, Br. Zool. Snowbird} \end{cases}$
Bunting. Snowflake, ibid. Snow-bunting. Faun. Am. Sept.
11.

Severn River, N° 24—26.

> The bird, in summer dress, corresponds exactly
> with the description of the greater brambling,
> Br. Zool. The description of the snowflake,
> or the same bird in winter dress, ibid. vol. IV
> p. 19. is somewhat different, perhaps owing
> to the different seasons the birds were caught
> in, as it is well known they change their co-
> lour gradually. They are the first of the mi-
> gratory birds, which come in spring to Severn
> settlement; in the year 1771 they appeared
> April the 11th, stayed about a month or five
> weeks, and then proceeded further northward
> in order to breed there; they return in Sep-
> tember, stay till the cold grows severe in
> November, then retire southward to a warmer
> climate. They live in flocks, feed on grass-
> seeds, and about the dunghills, are easily
> caught under a small net, some oatmeal being
> strewed under it to allure them; they are
> very fat, and fine eating. The weight is 1
> ounce and 5 drams, the length 6½ inches, and
> the breadth 10 inches.

EM BRIZA. 26. Leucophrys. *New Species*. White
Crowned Bunting.

Severn River, N° 50. Albany Fort, 10.

> This elegant little species of Bunting is called
> a hedge sparrow at Hudson's Bay, and has
> F f f 2   not

not hitherto been described. It visits Severn settlement in June, and feeds on grass-seeds, little worms, grubs, &c. It weighs $\frac{3}{4}$ of an ounce, and is $7\frac{1}{2}$ inches long, and 9 inches broad; the bill and legs are flesh-coloured; the male is not materially different from the female, its nests are built in the bottom of willow bushes, it lays three eggs of a chocolate colour. It visits Albany Fort in May, breeds there, and leaves it in September.

12. FRINGILLA, { 27. Lapponica. 317. 1. Faun.
   Finch. { Suec. 235.

Severn river, N° 52.

It is called *Tecurmashish,* by the natives at Hudson's Bay. The description in Linneus's Fauna Suecica coincides exactly with the specimen; that in his System answers very nearly: Mr. Brisson's description (though he quotes Linneus, and Linneus quotes him) is widely different. The specimen sent over is a female; the males have more of the ferruginous colour on the head; the eyes are blue, the legs dark brown. It is only a winter inhabitant near Severn river, appears not before November, and is commonly found among the juniper trees; it weighs $\frac{1}{2}$ of an ounce, its length is 5 inches, and its breadth 7.

FRINGILLA.

FRINGILLA.   28. Linaria.   322.   29.   Lesser red headed Linnet.   Br. Zool.

Severn River, N° 23.

> The descriptions of Linneus, Brisson, and the British Zoology, answer perfectly well.   The figure in Planche enluminée 151. f. 2. has a quite ferruginous back contrary to all the descriptions and the specimen before us, in which all the feathers on the back are dusky, edged with dirty white.

29. Montana, 324. 37.   Mountain Sparrow, Tree Sparrow. Br. Zool.   Edw. 269.   Brisson III. p. 79.   Faun. Am. Sept.

Severn River, N° 20.

> This seems to be a variety, as its tail is rather longer than usual, and forked; it answers nearly to the descriptions given by the ornithologists, and seems to be a female, as it has no black under the throat and eyes, and no white collar.   The bill and legs are black, the eyes blue.   At Severn settlement it arrives in May, goes to breed further northwards, and returns in autumn: the weight is ¾ of an ounce, the length 6½ inches, and breadth 10.   I was inclined to make this bird a new species, on account of the many differences between it and the mountain sparrow; but considering the specimen sent over was not in the best order, and might be a female, I thought it best to leave it where it is, till we are better informed.

FRIN-

FRINGILLA. 30. Hudsonias. *New Specimen.*
Severn River, N° 18.

> This is certainly a nondescript species; it only visits Severn settlement in summer, not being seen there before June, when it stays about a fortnight, goes further to the northward to breed, and passes by Severn again in autumn on its return south. It is very difficult to procure, and therefore it could not be determined whether the specimen was a male or female. It frequents the plains, and lives on grass-seeds; it weighs ½ an ounce, is 6¼ inches long, and 9 inches broad: it has a small blue eye, and a whitish bill faintly tinged with red; the whole body is blackish, or of a soot colour, the belly alone with the two outermost tail feathers on each side being white. It is to be wished that more specimens and circumstantial accounts of this bird were sent over, which would enable us to determine its character with more precision.

13. MUSCICAPA, { 31. Striata. *New Species,* Striped
Flycatcher. { Flycatcher.
Severn River, N° 48 and 49. Male and Female.

> This species visits Severn river only in summer, feeding on grass-seeds, etc.; it weighs half an ounce, is 5 inches long, and seven broad; the male is widely different from the female: this species is entirely nondescript.

2   14. MOTA-

14. MOTACILLA, { 32. Calendula. 337. 47. Ruby
    Wagtail. { crowned Wren. Edw. 254.
Faun. Am. Sept.

> (The number belonging to this bird is lost;
> however, it is most probably that sent from
> Severn river, N° 53.)

> It answers to the descriptions and the figure of
> Edwards; its weight is 4 drams, its length 4
> inches, and its breadth 5. It migrates, feeds
> on grass-seeds and the like, and breeds in the
> plains; the number of eggs is not known.

15. PARUS, { 33. Atricapillus. 341. 6. Black Cap
Titmouse. { Titmouse.

Albany Fort, N° 11.

> The description given by Linneus answers, and
> so does M. Brisson's in most particulars, ex-
> cept that the quill-feathers are not white on
> the inside. These birds stay at Albany Fort
> all the year, yet seem most numerous in the
> coldest weather; probably being then more
> in want of food, they come nearer the settle-
> ments, in order to pick up all remnants.
> They feed on flies and small maggots, and like-
> wise on the buds of the sprig-birch, in which
> they perhaps only search for insects; they
> make a twittering noise, from which the na-
> tive call them *Kiss-kiss-ke-shish*.

PARUS.

PARUS. 34. Hudsonicus. *New Species.* Hudson's Bay Titmouse.

Severn River, N° 12.

> This new species of titmouse, is called *Peche-ke-ke-shish*, by the natives. They are common about the juniper-bushes, of which the buds are their food; in winter they fly about from tree to tree in small flocks, the severest weather not excepted. They breed about the settlements, and lay 5 eggs; they have small eyes, with a white streak under them, and black legs: the male and female are quite alike; they weigh half an ounce, are $5\frac{1}{8}$ inches long, and 7 inches broad.

16. HIRUNDO,⎫ 35.
     Swallow. ⎭

Severn River, N° 58.

> The swallows build under the windows, and on the face of steep banks of the river, they disappear in autumn; and the Indians say, they were never found torpid under water, probably because they have no large nets to fish with under the ice. The specimen sent answers in some particulars to the description of the Martin, Hirundo Urbica, Linn. but seems to be smaller, and has no white on the rump. I have, therefore, thought it best to leave the species undetermined, till further informations are received from Hudson's Bay, on this subject.

2. WATER-

2. WATER-BIRDS.

VI. { GRALLÆ,
{ Clovenfooted.   Faun. Am. Sept.

17. ARDEA, { 36. Canadensis. 234. 3.   Edw. 133.
Heron. { Canada Crane. Faun. Am. Sept. 14.

Severn River, N° 35.   Blue Crane.

> The account from Severn settlement says, there
> is no material difference between the male
> and female; however, the specimen sent over,
> I take to be a female, as its plumage is in
> general duller than that figured by Edwards,
> and as the last row of white coverts of the wing
> are wanting. These cranes arrive near Severn
> in May, have only two young at a time,
> retire southward in autumn; frequent lakes
> and ponds, and feed on fish, worms, &c.
> They weigh seven pounds and a half, are
> 3¼ feet long, and 3 feet 5 inches broad; the
> bill is 4 inches long, the legs 7 inches, but
> the leg and thigh 19.

ARDEA.   37. Americana, 234. 5. Hooping Crane.
Edw. 132.   Catesby, l. 75.   Faun. Am. Sept.
14.

York Fort.

> Edwards's figure is very exact; Catesby's is not
> so good, as it represents the bill too thick to-
> wards the point.

38. Stellaris, 239. 21. *Varietas.* The Bittern, Br.
Zool. Edw. 136. Faun. Am. Sept. pag. 14 *.
Severn River, N° 64.

> At first sight, I thought the specimen sent from
> Hudson's Bay, was a young bird; but upon
> nearer examination and comparing it with
> Mr. Edwards's account and figure, I take it
> to be a variety of the common bittern pe-
> culiar to North America; it is smaller, but
> upon the whole very much resembles our
> bittern. Mr. Edwards's measurements and
> drawings correspond very well with the speci-
> men.

> This bird appears at Severn river the latter end
> of May, lives chiefly among the swamps and
> willows, where it builds its nest, and lays
> only two eggs at a time; it is very indolent,
> and, when roused, removes only to a short
> distance.

18. SCOLOPAX, { 39. Totanus. 245. 12. Spotted
Woodcock. { Woodcock. Faun. Am. Sept. 14.
Albany Fort, N° 16.

> This bird is called a yellow leg at Albany fort,
> from the bright yellow colour of the legs,
> especially in old birds; a circumstance, in
> which it varies from the descriptions of Lin-
> neus and Brisson, probably because they de-

---

* In the Faunula Americæ Septentrionalis, p. 14. the synonym
of Ardea Hudsonias, Linn. has by mistake been annexed to the
bittern, and likewise pl. 135 of Edwards has been quoted instead of plate 136. They are two very different birds.

scribed

scribed from dried specimens, in which the yellow colour always changes into brown. It agrees in other respects perfectly well with the descriptions: it comes to Albany fort in April or beginning of May, and leaves it the latter end of September. It feeds on small shell fish, worms, and maggots; and frequents the banks of rivers, swamps, &c. It is called by the natives *Sa-sa-shew*, from the noise it makes.

SCOLOPAX. 40. Lapponica. 246. 15. Red God-wit. Br. Zool. Faun. Am. Sept. 14. Ed. 138.

Churchill River, N° 13.

Linneus describes this bird very exactly in his Systema Naturæ: the middle of the belly has no white in the Society's specimen, as that had from which the description in the Br. Zool. octavo I. p. 353, 354, was taken. All the other characters correspond.

SCOLOPAX. 41. Borealis. *New Species*. Eskimaux Curlew. Faun. Am. Sept, 14.

Albany Fort, N° 15.

This species of Curlew, is not yet known to the ornithologists; the first mention is made of it in the Faunula Americæ Septentrionalis, or catalogue of North American animals. It is called *Wee-kee-me-nase-su*, by the natives; feeds on swamps, worms, grubs, &c; visits Albany Fort in April or beginning of May; breeds to the northward of it, returns in Au-

G g g 2 gust,

gust, and goes away southward again the latter end of September.

19. TRINGA, { 42. Interpres. 248. 4. Turnstone. Sand-piper. { Edw. 141. Faun. Am. Sept. 14.

Severn River, N° 31 and 32.

> This species is well described by the ornithologists; its weight is 3½ ounces, the length 8¾ inches, and the breadth 17 inches; it has four young at a time; its eyes are black, and the feet of a bright orange: this bird frequents the sides of the river.

43. Helvetica. 250. 12, Brisson. Av. V. p. 106. t. 10. f. 2.

> (The number was lost, perhaps it is N° 17, from Fort Albany; upon that supposition the account is as follows: "the natives call it " *Waw-pusk-abrea-shish*, or white bear bird; " it feeds on berries, insects, grubs, worms, " and small shell-fish; visits and leaves Al- " bany fort at the same time with the *Sco-* " *lopax Totanus*, and *Borealis*.")

> I find this bird answers very well to its description; the throat, breast, and upper part of the belly are blackish, as in the descriptions, but mixed with white lunulated spots, which are neither described nor expressed in M. Brisson's figure, and may be owing to the difference of sex, or climate.

VII.

VII. {ANSERES.
{Webbed-footed.   Faun. Am. Sept.

29. ANAS, {44. Marila. 196. 8. Scaup Duck. Br.
Duck, {Zool.   Faun. Am. Sept. 17.

Severn River, N° 44 and 45.   Fishing Ducks.

> Linneus's description, and the figure in the Br.
> Zoology, folio, plate Q. p. 153, agree per-
> fectly well with the specimens.   The female,
> as Linneus observes, is quite brown, the breast
> and upper part of the back being of a glossy
> reddish brown ; the speculum of the wing
> and the belly are white.   The eyes of the
> male have very bright yellow irides ; those
> of the female are of a faint dirty yellow.
> The female is two ounces heavier than the
> male, which weighs one pound and a half,
> is 16½ inches long, and 20 inches broad.

ANAS. 45. Nivalis. Snow Goose. Faun. Am. Sept.
p. 16.   Lawson's Carolina.   Anser niveus Briss.
VI. 288. Klein. Anser nivis. Schwenkfeld, Mar-
sigli. Danub. p. 802. t. 49.

Severn River, N° 40, and a young one, N° 41. white
Goose.

> These white geese are very numerous at Hud-
> son's Bay, many thousands being annually
> killed with the gun, for the use of the set-
> tlements.   They are usually shot whilst on
> the wing, the Indians being very expert at
> that exercise, which they learn from their
> youth ; they weigh five or six pounds, are
> 2⅔ feet

2⅔ feet long, and 3½ broad; their eyes are black, the irides small and red, the legs likewise red; they feed along the sea, and are fine eating; their young are bluish grey, and do not attain a perfect whiteness till they are a year old. They visit Severn river first in the middle of May, on their journey northward, where they breed; return in the beginning of September, with their young, staying at Severn settlement about a fortnight each time. The Indian name is *Way-way*, at Churchill river. Linneus has not taken notice of this species.

ANAS. 46. Canadensis. 198. 14. Canada Goose. Faun. Am. Sept. 16. Edw. 151. Catesby I. 92, &c.

Severn River, N° 42.

The Canada geese are very plentiful at Hudson's Bay, great quantities of them are salted, but they have a fishy taste. The specimen sent over agrees perfectly with the descriptions and drawings. At Hudson's Bay this species is called the *Small Grey Goose*. Besides this, and the preceding white goose, Mr. Graham, the gentleman who sent the account from Severn settlement, mentions three other species of wild geese to be met with at Hudson's Bay; he calls them,

1. The large Grey Goose.
2. The Blue Goose.
3. The Laughing Goose.

4

The

The first of these, the large grey goose, he says,
is so common in England, that he thought
it unnecessary to send specimens of it over. It
is however presumed, that though Mr. Graham has shewn himself a careful observer,
and an indefatigable collector ; yet, not being
a naturalist, he could not enter into any mi-
nute examination about the species to which
each goose belongs, nor from mere recollec-
tion know, that his grey goose was actually
to be met with in England. A natural his-
torian, by examination, often finds material
differences, which would escape a person un-
acquainted with natural history. The wish,
therefore, of seeing the specimens of these
species of geese, must occur to every lover
of that science. Mr. Graham says, the large
grey geese are the only species that breed
about Severn river. They frequent the plains
and swamps along the coast. Their weight
is nine pounds.

The blue goose is as big as the white goose ;
and the laughing goose is of the size of the
Canada or small grey goose. These two
last species are very common along Hudson's
Bay to the southward, but very rare to the
northward of Severn river. The Indians
have a peculiar method of killing all these
species of geese, and likewise swans. As
these birds fly regularly along the marshes,
the Indians range themselves in a line across
the marsh, from the wood to high water
mark, about musket shot from each other,
so

so as to be sure of intercepting any geese which fly that way. Each person conceals himself, by putting round him some brush wood; they likewise make artificial geese of sticks and mud, placing them at a short distance from themselves, in order to decoy the real geese within shot: thus prepared, they sit down, and keep a good look out; and as soon as the flock approaches, they all lie down, imitating the call or note of geese, which these birds no sooner hear, and perceive the decoys, than they go straight down towards them; then the Indians rise on their knees, and discharge one, two or three guns each, killing two or even three geese at each shot, for they are very expert. Mr. Graham says, he has seen a row of Indians, by calling round a flock of geese, keep them hovering among them, till every one of the geese was killed. Every species of geese has its peculiar note or call, which must greatly increase the difficulty of enticing them.

ANAS. 47. Albeola. 199. 18. The Red Duck. Faun. Am. Sept. 17. Edw. t. 100. Sarcelle de la Louisiane. Brisson VI. t. 41. f. 1.

Severn River, N° 37 and 38. Fishing Birds.

The descriptions and figures answer very well with the male, except that the three exterior feathers are not white on the outside, but all dusky.

The female is not described by any one of the ornithologists; and therefore deserves to be noticed,

3

noticed, to prevent future mistakes. The whole bird is dusky, a few feathers on the forehead are rusty, and some about the ears of a dirty white; the breast is grey, the belly and speculum in the wings white; the bill and legs are black. They visit Severn settlement in June, build their nests in trees, and breed among the woods, and near ponds; the weight of the female is one pound, its length 14 inches, and its breath 21.

ANAS. 48. Clangula. 201. 23. Golden Eye. Br. Zool. Faun. Am. Sept. 16.

Severn River, N° 51.

These birds frequent lakes and ponds, and breed there: they eat fish and slime, and cannot rise off the dry land. The legs and irides are yellow; their weight is 2⅜ pounds, and their measure 19 inches in length, and two feet in breadth. The specimen sent is the male.

ANAS. 49. Perspicillata. 201. 25. Black Duck. Faun. Am. Sept. 16. Edw. 155.

Churchill River, N° 14.

This species is exactly described, and well drawn by Edwards. The Indians call it *She ke-su-partem*. It ought to come into the first division of Linneus's ducks, "rostro basi "gibbo," as its bill is really very unequal at the base.

ANAS. 50. Glacialis. 203. 30, and Hyemalis, 202. 29. Edw. t. 156. Swallow-tail. Br. Zool. Faun. Am. Sept. 17.

Churchill River, N° 12.

At Churchill River the Indians call this species, *Har-har-vey*; it corresponds with Edwards's description and drawing, plate 156, but differs much from Linneus's inexact description of the Anas Hyemalis, to which he, however, quotes Edwards. Upon the whole it is almost without a doubt that the bird represented by Edwards, plate 280, and Br. Zool. folio, plate Q. 7, and quoted by Linneus for his Anas glacialis, is the male, and that the bird figured by Edwards t. 156, and quoted by Linneus for the Anas Hyemalis, is the female, of one and the same species. Linneus mentions a white body (in his Anas hyemalis) which in Edw. Tab. 156, and in the Society's specimen, is all brown and dusky, except the belly, temples, a spot on the back of the head, and the sides of the rump, which are white. Linneus says, that the temples are black; in the specimen now sent over, and in Mr. Edwards's figure, which Linneus quotes, they are white; the breast, back, and wings, are not black as he says, but rather brown and dusky. A further proof, that Linneus's Anas Glacialis and Hyemalis are the same, is that the feet in both t. 156 and 280 of Edwards are red, and the bill black, with an orange spot.

ANAS.

ANAS. 51. Crecca. 204. 33. *Varietas.* Teal.
Br. Zool. Faun. Am. Sept. 17.

Severn River, N° 33, 34. Male and female.

This is a variety of the teal, for it wants the
two white streaks above and below the eyes;
the lower one indeed is faintly expressed in
the male, which has also a lunated bar of
white over each shoulder; this is not to be
found in the European teal. This species is
not very plentiful near Severn river; they
live in the woods and plains near little ponds
of water, and have from five to seven young
at a time.

ANAS. 52. Histrionica. 204. 35. Harlequin Duck.
Faun. Am. Sept. 16. Edw. t. 99.

This bird had no number fixed to it; it agrees
perfectly with Edwards's figure.

ANAS. 53. Boschas. 205. 40. Mallard Drake.
Faun. Am. Sept. Br. Zool.

Severn River, N° 39.

It is called Stock Drake at Hudson's Bay, and
corresponds in every respect with the European one, upon comparison.

21. PELECANUS,⎫ 54. Onocrotalus. 251. 1. *A va-*
Pelecan. ⎭ *riety.*

York Fort.

This variety of the pelecan, agrees in every pa-
ticular with Linneus's oriental pelecan (Pele-
H h h 2   canus

canus onocrotalus orientalis), but has a peculiar tuft or fringe of fibres in the middle
of the upper mandible, something nearer the
apex than the base. This tuft has not been
mentioned by any author, and is likewise
wanting in Edwards's pelican, t. 92. with
which the Society's specimen corresponds in
every other circumstance. The P. Onocrotalus occidentalis, Linn. or Edw. t. 93
American pelican, is very different from it:
the chief differences are the colour, which
in our Hudson's Bay bird is white, but in
Edwards's is of a greyish brown; and the
size, which in the white bird is almost double
of the brown one. The quill-feathers are
black, and the shafts of the larger ones white.
The *Alula*, or bastard wing, is black. The
bill and legs are yellow.

22. COLYMBUS. } 55. Glacialis. 221. 5. Northern
  * Diver, } Diver. Br. Zool. Faun. Am.
Sept. 16.

Churchill River, N° 8. called a Loon there.

This bird is well described and drawn in the
British Zoology, in folio.

  * * } 56. Auritus, *a.* 222. 8. Edw. 145.
Grebe. } Eared Grebe. Faun. Am. Sept. 15.

Severn River, N° 43.

This is exactly the bird drawn by Edwards, t.
145. The specimen sent over is a female.
It differs much from our lesser crested Grebe.
  Br.

Br. Zool. octavo I. p. 396, and Br. Zool. illustr. plate 77. fig. 2. and Ed. 96. fig. 2. However, in both these works, it is looked on only as a variety, or different in sex. Mr. Graham has the same opinion. It lives on fish, frequenting the lakes near the sea coast. It lays its eggs in water, and cannot rise off dry land. It is seen about the beginning of June, but migrates southward in autumn. It is called *Sekeep*, by the natives. Its eyes are small, the irides red; it weighs one pound, and measures one foot in length, and one third more in breadth.

23. LARUS.} 57. Parasiticus. 226. 10. Arctic Gull. Gull.} Br. Zool. Faun. Am. Sept. 16. Edw. 148. 149.

Churchill River, N° 15.

This species is called a *Man of War*, at Hudson's Bay. It seems to be a female, by the dirty white colour of its plumage below; it agrees very well with Edwards's drawing, and that in the Br. Zool. illustr.

24. STERNA.} 58. Hirundo (*Variety*), 227. 2. Tern.} The greater Tern. Br. Zool. Faun. Am. Sept.

(The number belonging to this bird is lost, perhaps it is N° 17, from Churchill River, called "A sort

" A sort of Gull, called Egg-breakers, by
" the natives.")

The feet are black; the tail is shorter and
much less forked than that described and
drawn in the Br. Zool. The outermost tail-
feather likewise wants the black, which that
in the British Zoology has. In other respects it is the same.

DESCRIP-

DESCRIPTIONES Avium Rariorum
e Sinu Hudsonis.

1. Falco sacer.

Falco, cerâ pedibusque coeruleis, corpore, remigibus rectricibusque fuscis, fasciis pallidis ; capite, pectore & abdomine albis, maculis longitudinalibus fuscis.

Habitat ad sinum Hudsonis et in reliqua America Septentrionali ; victitat Lagopodibus & Tetraonum speciebus.

Descr. *Magnitudo* Corvi.

Rostrum, cera, pedes coerulea ; rostrum breve, curvum, coeruleo-atrum ; mandibula utraque, basi pallide coerulea, apice nigrescente, utraque emarginata.

Caput tectum pennis albidis, maculis longitudinalibus, fuscis.

Oculi magni ; irides flavæ.

Gula alba, fusco-maculata.

Dorsum et tectrices alarum, plumis fuscis, ferrugineo-pallide marginatis, maculatisque, maculis rachin non attingentibus.

Pectus, venter, crissum, tectrices alarum inferiores, & femora alba, maculis longitudinalibus nigro-fuscis.

Remiges fusco-nigri, viginti duo ; primores apicibus margine albis, maculis ferrugineo-

3

rugineo-pallidis, intra majoribus, transversis, extra minoribus, rotundatis.

Rectrices duodecim, supra fuscæ, fasciis
circiter duodecim & apice albidis ; infra
cinereæ, fasciis albidis.

2. STRIX NEBULOSA.

STRIX capite lævi, corpore fusco, albido undulatim
striato, remige sexto longiore, apice nigricante.
Habitat circa Sinum Hudsonis, victitat Leporibus,
Lagopodibus, Muribusque.

DESCR. *Rostrum* fusco-flavum, mandibula superiore
superius magis flava.

Oculi magni, iridibus flavis.

Caput facie cinerea, e pennis fusco et pallide cinereo alternatim striatis. Pone
hasce pennas collum versus est ordo
plumularum fuscarum ad utramque ge-
nam, semicirculum nigrum efficiens.

Occiput, cervix, et collum fusca, pennis,
marginibus albo-maculatis.

Pectus albidum, maculis longitudinalibus
transversisque fuscis.

Abdomen album, superius uti pectus maculis longitudinalibus, sed inferius striis
transversis notatum.

Dorsum totum et tectrices alæ, caudæque
confertim ex fusco & albido undulato-
striatæ.

Alæ fuscæ ; remiges primores fusci, griseo
transversim fasciati, fasciis latis nebulosis.
Remex sextus, reliquis longior, apice
magis

I

magis nigricans; primus vero reliquis primoribus brevior. Remiges reliqui pallidiores, obscurius fasciati. .

Cauda rotundata, rectricibus duodecim: duæ intermediæ paullo longiores, totæ cinerascente albido fuscoque undulatim striatæ, lineis duplicatis fuscis transversis pluribus. Rectrices reliquæ fuscæ albido substriatæ.

Pedes tecti pennis albidis fusco-striatis.

Magnitudo fere Strigis Nycteæ, Linn.

Longitudo unciarum 16 pedis Anglicani.

Latitudo pedum quatuor.

Pondus librarum trium.

3. TETRAO PHASIANELLUS.

Linn. Ed. X. p. 160. n. 5.

TETRAO pedibus hirsutis, cauda cuneiformi, remigibus nigris, exterius albo-maculatis.

Habitat ad Sinum Hudsonis.

DESCR. *Magnitudo* fere Tetraonis Tetricis. Linn.

Rostrum nigrum.

Oculorum irides avellaneæ.

Caput, collum & dorsum testacea, nigro transversim fasciata : macula albida inter rostrum et oculos : latera colli notata maculis rotundatis albidis.

Dorsum testaceum, plumis omnibus late nigro-fasciatis.

Uropygium magis albido-cinereum, nigredine fimbriata secundum rachin plumarum.

Pectus & Venter albida, maculis cordatis fusco-testaceis in ventre saturatioribus.

Alarum tectrices dilute testaceo, nigro, alboque transversim fasciatæ, maculis pluribus rotundis albis. *Remiges* primores nigri, latere exteriore albo-maculati ; secundarii fusci, apice & ad marginem exteriorem albo subfasciati : postremi vero testaceo fasciati, apice tantum albi.

Rectrices breves, exteriores pallide fuscæ, apice albæ, duæ intermediæ reliquis longiores, testaceo-maculatæ.

Pedes plumis albo-griseis vesti digitis pectinatis.

Longitudo unciarum 16 pedis Anglicani.

Latitudo pedum duorum.

4. EMBERIZA LEUCOPHRYS *.

EMBERIZA remigibus rectricibusque fuscis, capite nigro, fascia verticis, superciliisque niveis.

Habitat in America Boreali ad Sinum Hudsonis.

DESCR. *Magnitudo* circiter *fringillæ cœlibis.*

Rostrum rubrum, s. carnei coloris : Nares subrotundæ.

Caput fascia verticali lata candida, paululum ante rostrum desinente ; fascia atra

---

* Λευκòς albus. Ôφρὺς supercilium.

I

lata

lata ad utrumque latus fasciæ albæ. Su-
percilia alba, desinentia in lineas, fasciam
albam verticalem adtingentes ; arcus dein
atri, ex angulis oculorum, fere in occi-
pite confluentes.

Collum cinerascens, in pectore dilutius.

Dorsum ferrugineo-fuscum, marginibus
plumularum cinereis.

Alæ fuscæ ; remigum primorum margines
exteriores tenuissimi pallidi, interiores
cinerascentes : secundarii & pennæ tectrices fuscæ, marginibus latiusculis, versus apicem albis, efficientibus fasciam
albam ; super quam fascia altera alba ex
maculis albis in apice tectricum mino-
rum, s. plumarum scapularium. Alulæ
albæ. Remiges subtus cinerei, marginibus albis.

Pectus cinereum, abdomen dilutius, fere
album.

Crissum & plumulæ femora tegentes lutes-
centia.

Uropygium cinereo-fuscum.

Cauda æqualis ; rectrices duodecim fuscæ,
marginibus paullo pallidioribus, subtus
cinereæ.

Pedes carnei coloris, digito intermedio &
ungue postico reliquis longioribus.

Longitudo unciarum 7 pedis Anglicani.

Latitudo inter alas extensas 9 unciarum
pedis Anglicani.

Cauda partem tertiam longitudinis totius
aviculæ efficit.

Alæ complicatæ paululum ultra caudæ exortum protenduntur.

Pondus drachmarum sex.

5. Fringilla Hudsonias.

Fringilla fusco-cinerascens, rostro albido, pectore inferiore, abdomine, reċtricibusque quatuor extremis albis.

Habitat in America Boreali.

Descr. *Magnitudo* circiter fringillæ carduelis.

Rostrum albidum, rubedine aliqua imbutum.

Oculi parvi, cœrulei.

Corpus totum cinereo-nigricans, s. potius fuliginosum.

Peċlus inferius & *abdomen* alba.

Remiges fusci, cinereo-marginati : alæ complicatæ mediam fere caudam adtingunt.

Reċlrices fuscæ, extimæ utrinque duæ totæ albæ, tertia fusca, macula oblonga alba, ad latus interius, prope rachin, apicem attingens ; reliquæ totæ fuscæ.

Pondus semunciæ.

Longitudo unciarum 6¼ pedis Anglicani.

Latitudo unciarum novem.

6. Muscicapa striata.

Muscicapa cinereo-virens, dorso nigro striato, subtus flavescenti-alba, gula lateribusque peċtoris fusco maculatis.

Habitat

Habitat ad Sinum Hudsonis.

Quum mas à fœmina multum differat, utique congruum est, utrumque sexum separatim describere.

DESCR. Mas.

Rostrum trigonum, mandibu superiore paululum longiore, ante apicem leviter emarginata, nigra ; inferiore basi flavescente.

Nares subrotundæ.

Vibrissæ nigræ.

Caput supra totum atrum ad oculos usque. *Genæ* à rostro in occiput totæ albæ ; occiput albo & nigro variegatum.

Gula flavescenti-alba maculis fuscis.

Pectus albidum, lateribus, sive versus occiput maculis nigris variegatum.

Dorsum cinereo-virens, striis sive maculis longitudinalibus nigris latioribus, è plumulis nigris, margine virentibus.

Abdomen album.

Uropygium cinereum, nigro-maculatum.

Alæ fuscæ ; remiges primores pallido marginati, secundarii apice tenuissimo albo ; duæ ultimæ margine exteriore albo ; tectrices fuscæ, majores flavescenti albo, minores candido in apice maculatæ, unde fasciæ albæ binæ in alis.

Cauda fusca ; rectrix utrinque prima s. extima, latere interiore macula magna alba, marginem interiorem attingente ; proxima s. secunda macula oblonga minore alba, etiam marginem interiorem attingente ;

attingente ; utrinque tertia, latere interiore versus apicem albo-marginata.

Pedes lutei ; ungues breves, pallide fusci.

Magnitudo circiter *Pari atricapilli* ; Linn.

Longitudo 5 unciarum.

Latitudo 7 unciarum pedis Anglicani.

Fœmina.

Rostrum, alæ, cauda, abdomen, uropygium, pedes & mensuræ ut in mare.

Caput flavo-virens, striis brevibus tenui-
busque longitudinalibus nigris ; linea fla-
vissima à basi rostri incipiens super oculos
ducta ; palpebræ flavæ.

Gula, genæ & pectus albido-flava ; maculæ
sparsæ oblongiusculæ fuscæ, ab utroque
oris angulo usque in pectoris latera.

Dorsum, ut in mare, sed viridius, & striæ
nigræ minores.

7. PARUS HUDSONICUS.

PARUS capite fusco-rubescente, dorso cinereo, jugulo
atro, fascia suboculari, pectoreque albis, hypo-
chondriis rufis.

Habitat ad Sinum Hudsonis.

DESCR. *Rostrum* subulatum, integerrimum, atrum,
basi è regione narium tectum fasciculis
setarum ferruginearum, lineas 4 (unciæ
pedis Anglicani) longum.

Caput fusco-ferrugineum, fascia sub oculis
alba ; gula atra, nigredine extensa sub
hac fascia alba.

Dorsum

Dorsum cinereo-virens, è plumis longioribus, fuscis, apice tantum cinereo-viren-
tibus, s. olivaceis.

Pectus & Abdomen alba, sed plumæ omnes
basi nigræ, apice tantum albæ.

Latera abdominis & lumbi ferruginei.

Alæ fuscæ, remigum margine omni cinereo.

Cauda fusca, rotundata, rectricibus 12,
margine cinereis.

Uropygium tectum plumulis aliquot nigris,
apice albido-rufis.

Pedes nigri; digitus posticus cum ungue
anticorum digitorum medio, duplo longior.

Longitudo unciarum 5⅛ pedis Anglicani.

Latitudo unciarum 7.

Cauda uncias 2½ longa.

8. SCOLOPAX BOREALIS.

SCOLOPAX rostro arcuato, pedibusque nigris, corpore
fusco, griseo-maculato, subtus ochroleuco.

Habitat in Sinus Hudsonis inundatis, & pratis hu-
midis, victitans vermibus & insectis : mense Aprili
vel initio Maii primum visa est, circa Castellum
Albany, inde in terras magis arcticas migrat, ibique
nidificat; redit ad idem castellum mense Au-
gusto; regiones Australiores petit circa finem Sep-
tembris.

Affinis scolopace arquata Linn. sed differt corpore triplo minore, rostro ratione corporis
breviore,

breviore, colore in dorso saturate fusco, in abdomine ochroleuco.

DESCR. *Caput* pallidum, lineolis confertis longitudinalibus fuscis: sinciput saturate fuscum, pallido maculatum.

Rostrum nigricans, arcuatum, longitudine duarum unciarum pedis Anglicani, mandibula inferiore basi rufa.

Collum, pectus, abdomen & crissum ochroleuca; pectore colloque lineolis longitudinalibus fuscis confertioribus, abdomine & crisso fere nullis, vel tenuibus notatis.

Femora semi-tecta plumulis ochroleucis, fusco maculatis.

Latera abdominis sub alis præsertim, rufa, pennis transversim fusco fasciatis.

Dorsum totum saturate fuscum, pennis margine albido griseis.

Alæ fuscæ; remiges primores immaculati, primores rachi tota alba; reliqui, s. secundarii pallide griseo-marginati. Tectrices late griseo-marginatæ. Tectrices inferiores alæ, ferrugineæ fusco transversim fasciatæ. Alæ complicatæ fere mediam caudam attingunt.

Uropygium fuscum, marginibus maculisque pennarum albidis.

Cauda brevis, fusca, rectricibus albido transversim fasciatis.

Pedes nigri, s. cœrulescentes.
Longitudo unciarum 13½.
Latitudo circiter unciarum 21.

3   9. ANAS

9. ANAS NIVALIS.

ANAS, rostro cylindrico, corpore albo, remigibus primoribus nigris.

Habitat in America Boreali, per Sinum Hudsonis migrans.

DESCR. *Corpus* totum album, magnitudine anseris domestici nostratis.

Rostrum luteum, mandibulis subserratis.

Oculi iride rubra.

Remiges decem primores nigri, scapis albis : tectrices infimæ cinereæ, scapis nigris ; pennæ duæ alulæ, itidem cinereæ, scapis nigris.

Pedes rubri.

Longitudo pedum duorum & unciarum octo.

Latitudo pedum 3½.

Pondus librarum 5 vel 6.

𝔆𝔞𝔪𝔟𝔯𝔦𝔡𝔤𝔢 :
PRINTED BY C. J. CLAY AND SON,
AT THE UNIVERSITY PRESS.

𝕿𝖍𝖊 𝖂𝖎𝖑𝖑𝖚𝖌𝖍𝖇𝖞 𝕾𝖔𝖈𝖎𝖊𝖙𝖞

FOR THE

REPRINTING OF SCARCE ORNITHOLOGICAL WORKS.

ESTABLISHED 1879.

Committee of Selection:

ALFRED NEWTON, M.A., F.R.S., V.P.Z.S.
OSBERT SALVIN, M.A., F.R.S., F.Z.S.
PHILIP LUTLEY SCLATER, M.A., F.R.S., Sec. Z.S.
THE PAST AND PRESENT EDITORS OF "THE IBIS."

Director:

W. B. TEGETMEIER, F.Z.S.
FINCHLEY, N.

Secretary:

F. DU CANE GODMAN, F.L.S.
CHANDOS-STREET, CAVENDISH-SQUARE, LONDON, W.

THE WILLUGHBY SOCIETY.

At a Meeting of Ornithologists, at 6, Tenterden-street, Hanover-square, on May 7, 1879, Professor NEWTON in the Chair, it was agreed "That an Association should be formed for reprinting certain Ornithological Works interesting for their utility or rarity."

The late and present EDITORS of "The Ibis" and Mr TEGETMEIER were requested to form an Organising Committee to promote this object, and Mr F. GODMAN to act as Secretary.

The Committee thus appointed met at 11, Hanover-square, on June 4, 1879, when it was agreed :—

I. "That this Association be called 'THE WILLUGHBY SOCIETY for the reprinting of scarce Ornithological Works.'"

II. "That the Annual Subscription be £1, payable to the Secretary."

III. "That no Copies of Works reprinted by THE WILLUGHBY SOCIETY be sold."

IV. "That every Member of THE WILLUGHBY SOCIETY shall be entitled to one Copy of each Work printed in the year for which he shall subscribe."

In order to carry out effectually the object of this Society, it is necessary that the number of Members should be as large as possible : those, therefore, who wish to join it are requested to communicate with the Secretary, Mr F. D. GODMAN, 10, Chandos-street, Cavendish-square, W.C.

The following works have been already issued by the Society :—

For the Subscribers of the year 1880.

TUNSTALL'S "Ornithologia Britannica." Edited by Professor Newton, F.R.S.

DESFONTAINES' "Mémoire sur quelques nouvelles espèces d'oiseaux des côtes de Barbarie," from "Hist. de l'Acad. des Sciences," 1787. Edited by Professor Newton, F.R.S.

SIR ANDREW SMITH'S "Miscellaneous Ornithological Papers." Edited by Os. Salvin, F.R.S.

A. A. H. LICHTENSTEIN'S "Catalogus rerum naturalium rarissimarum." Hamburg: 1793. Edited by W. B. Tegetmeier, F.Z.S.

The Willughby Society.

For the Subscribers of the year 1881.

Scopoli's "Deliciæ Floræ et Faunæ Insubricæ" (the portion relating to birds). Edited by Professor Newton, F.R.S.

Forster's "Catalogue of the Animals of North America." Edited by P. L. Sclater, F.R.S.

Forster's "Account of Birds sent from Hudson's Bay." Edited by P. L. Sclater, F.R.S.

Leach's Catalogue of the Mammalia and Birds in the British Museum. Edited by W. B. Tegetmeier, F.Z.S.

The following works are under consideration as suitable to the operations of the Society.

Wagler's Ornithological papers from the "Isis."

Hodgson's papers in the "Indian Review" and "Asiatic Researches."

Savigny and Audouin's Ornithology of Egypt. The complete text in 8vo.

Vieillot's "Analyse d'une nouvelle ornithologie."

Barrère's "Ornithologiæ specimen novum."

Möhring's "Avium genera."

Bechstein's papers in the "Naturforscher."

Temminck's "Catalogue Systématique du Cabinet d'Ornithologie."

Sganzin's "Notes sur l'Ornithologie de Madagascar," from the Mém. de la Soc. d'Hist. Nat. de Strasbourg.

Ornithological papers by Ray and Lister in the "Philosophical Transactions."

Schwenckfeld's "Aviarium Silesiacum."

Ornithological papers in the Transactions of the Academy of Sciences of St Petersburg.

Ornithological portion of the Appendices to the "Reise" of Pallas. S. G. Gmelin, and other Russian Travellers.

Charleton's "Onomasticon."

Turner's "Avium &c. brevis et succincta Historia."

Barton's "Fragments of the Natural History of Pensylvania."

&c., &c.

www.ingramcontent.com/pod-product-compliance
Lightning Source LLC
Chambersburg PA
CBHW031320280626
47169CB00019B/2512